Object Impermanence

Weird and Fantastic Stories

Margery Bayne

The characters and events portrayed in this book are fictitious. Any similarity to real persons, living or dead, is coincidental and not intended by the author.

Copyright © 2022 Margery Bayne

All rights reserved.

No part of this book may be reproduced or used in any manner without written permission of the copyright holder except for the use of quotations in book reviews.

ISBN: 9798361708529

Cover design by: Andrew Rainnie

There's nothing under your bed. Nothing in your closet. Nothing waiting in the hall. You are surrounded by nothing.
You cannot escape it.

- Cecil, "Welcome to Nightvale"

STORIES

Unfinished Business	1
The Pawnshop of Intangible Things	5
The Lunch Cart Diner Special	10
Through the Glass Darkly	13
Object Impermanence	26
Die Beautiful	29
Another Life	31
Robot Bride	43
Barter for the Stars	45
Planning Advice for Your Last Days on Earth	48
Creek Monsters	49
Spiraling	53
What You Make Of It	55

UNFINISHED BUSINESS

"There he is. Go on now. Punch him," Remmie said as she hovered over Anne's shoulder, as she had since last Tuesday. The perils of being a medium. Ghosts hovered, haunted, howled, and — in this particular case — annoyed.

Anne had done her research. Having seen the dead since puberty and competently handling them since twenty-one, she was no slouch at this line of work. By all accounts, Remmie shouldn't be a ghost at all. Anne had checked out her obituary and her old Facebook page that was still active with loved ones' care-reaction-filled messages. Remmie hadn't been murdered, hadn't died suddenly, and — although young in the halls of unliving — she shouldn't have unfinished business.

She had died of cancer. A long, drawn-out battle with cancer. And, yes, Anne wasn't heartless; it was sad. But people who died of long, drawn-out battles with cancer had time to get their affairs in order, to say what they needed to say, and to have whatever needed to be heard said back to them in return.

Honestly, other than passing away in your sleep at a content one hundred years old, there wasn't a more foolproof way to pass over.

Anne's evidence: In all her years of communicating with the dead, she had never once before had a ghost of someone who had died of a long, drawn-out battle with cancer.

Remmie must've been emotionally incompetent in life. Anne didn't know why she had to be the one to suffer for it.

"I'm not going to punch some random man outside a Starbucks in broad daylight."

"Then why'd you come all the way here?"

"Because you wouldn't leave me to my afternoon of binge-watching *Frasier* reruns in peace. I'm here so you'll shut up."

"I'll shut up for good if you punch him. Pass on. You know, die for real."

Anne adjusted her sunglasses against her nose. It wasn't an overly bright day, but if she was going to scope out a stranger, she didn't need her staring to be obvious. An old trick for an occupational hazard.

"What did he do?"

"Does it matter?" Remmie's voice spoke directly into Anne's ear. It was unnecessary. Whispering in public might've been needed between mediums and ghosts of the past to not inspire suspicions against the medium's sanity. In the age of Bluetooth, overhearing only one-half of a conversation was normal.

"I might not be so opposed to punching him if I had the appropriate motivation."

"He deserves it," Remmie said. "Is that appropriate motivation?"

"I'm going to need more details."

"Unfortunately, I can't give them to you."

Anne crossed her arms. "I've had some of your lot try that on me before. There's no magic keeping your lips sealed. You're just lying."

"Your lot?"

Anne couldn't very well say "ghosts" in her one-half public conversation. There was only so far that line could be pushed. But she also wouldn't be accused of discrimination at this junction, when she was the one taking on all this emotional labor from the goodness of her heart and to the detriment of her binge-watching plans.

"Just..." Something in Remmie's voice cracked a little bit. Or it could've been her temporal presence in this plane of existence wavering. In either case, it caused Anne's stiffened shoulders to drop. "Can you walk over closer to him? You'll see what you need to see then."

Anne, empathic bitch that she was, jaywalked herself across the street. The man, who sat at one of those two-seater iron-wrought table-and-chair sets out on the sidewalk, didn't seem overtly douchey, although appearances could be deceiving. He sipped at a Venti-size whatever and wasn't even looking at his phone, the weirdo.

Suspicious, Anne supposed, if she made a mental stretch as intense as a straddle split.

"Closer," Remmie urged.

At this point, Anne had no other grounds to refuse. She was here, and she had already paid for parking.

Pretending that she was moseying her way into the Starbucks, Anne got closer. When she was just passing by the man, Remmie pushed.

There's a lot to be said about ghosts, intangibility, and how they interact with the world of the living. What needs to be known here was that Anne, being in communication with the dead, made her more able to touch and be touched by said subsect of the undead population.

Anne tripped right into the man's lap, rattling the tiny table, and sending the Venti-whatever to the cement.

The man caught her. "Woah there. Are you alright? Did you trip?"

Anne was confused. Betrayed. Incensed. She looked up. The man had the deepest brown eyes; she was a sucker for that.

"I — I — I —" She was also inane, apparently. She needed to finish this sentence. "I spilled your coffee."

"It's alright." He helped right her. Guided her to the other chair in the set. "Are you okay?"

"I owe you a coffee."

"I think I should get you a coffee. Can't have you so tired you're tripping into strangers in the street."

Anne laughed. It came out as a giggle. She was still inane, obviously, but that smile…

"Seriously," the man said. "What's your order? I'll run inside."

Anne rattled it off, even though she couldn't feel her face at the moment.

The man disappeared inside.

When Anne blinked, Remmie was still floating there.

"He promised me he would date again, but he's shit at keeping promises, apparently. So, I had to take matters into my own cold, undead hands. Bye." Remmie faded out of existence, even as Anne gaped, desperate to get in some final nasty words of revenge. None came.

The man returned quickly. When he handed her the drink, their fingers brushed, a zap of static electricity stinging between them.

Oh my, Anne realized, this was a new experience. She had been just set up by a ghost.

THE PAWNSHOP OF INTANGIBLE THINGS

You don't find the door until you stop looking for it. You had paced the block three times, crumpling the address-bearing napkin tighter in your fist with each passing. Your unusually patient, midday barstool companion must have gotten the numbers mixed up. That, or this was a wild goose chase of a joke.

Then you see it, about ten steps away, right off the sidewalk. The address numbers are painted in gold on the top of the door; under it is "LUCK's PAWN" in free hand. The whole thing is sun-bleached. It should have jumped out immediately against the modern, corporate background of the rest of this street.

There are no windows, so you knock two knuckles against the wood. No response. No business hours are posted. You try to the doorknob with the fading boldness of tipsiness that had led you all the way here. The door is unlocked.

Inside is a long, narrow room, with glaring fluorescent lights and a motley-colored carpet that might have been ripped right out of your dentist's waiting room.

What's most unusual are the jars lining three walls on floor-to-ceiling shelving: mason, canning, squat vials with stoppers, and even a few recorked wine bottles sticking up above the rest.

You lean in to inspect but don't step any closer. It's more than a "you break it, you buy it" fear. It's the unsettled feeling in your gut. Inside each jar is a coil of paper.

"Can I help you?" says an interrupting voice. You jolt in surprise.

Behind a jewelry counter at the very far end of the room stands a woman whom you cannot say for sure was there upon your entrance or not.

You clear your throat, but your voice still comes out higher than you want. "I heard you pay for ideas…?"

Outloud, no longer so dizzy with drink and desperation after bemoaning at the bar for the fourth time this week, it sounds like someone had pulled a real good one over on you.

The woman scoffs. "That is *such* a simplification." She rounds the counter and leans against the edge. "What I do is deal in intangibles."

A dozen questions immediately pop into your skull, but you don't raise a single one, not even a succinct "What?" The woman, however, must read it from your expression.

"Hopes, dreams, ambitions, inspirations, emotions." She rolls her wrist in the air. Your eyes follow her wine-colored fingernails. After you leave, it will be the one finite thing about her appearance you'll be sure of. "The stronger, the better. Love, hate, passion, conviction, and yes… ideas."

She walks to where the shelves meet in the left corner. "This is my collection of unwritten novels. I call it the slush pile… publishing joke." She points to a blue glass vial, and says in a stage whisper, "I think this one would've been great."

A book idea is what your bar companion had said he sold. He had gotten five hundred bucks. It seemed too good to be true, but valid enough of an exchange. Nothing as bizarre as this jar-covered room.

The woman shuffles to the right and touches the shelf above her head. "Religious doubts… faith, though, is hard to come by. Most people willing to sell it have already lost it."

She gives a tour of the room, labeling all of her oddities. "Reoccurring dreams — a lot of tidal waves" and "Ah — the memories. Memories are tricky ones. Have to be plucked like a daisy from a field. But they're the most… distinct."

Once she completes her tour and returns behind the counter, you say, "I don't get it."

She sighs in an overdramatic fashion. "It's simple. You sign over ownership of whatever intangible in question you're pawning or selling in exchange for cash."

You blink. "I sign a piece of paper, and you give me money."

"You sign away your intangible and I give you money, yes."

You say, "I need…" Lucky math is your strong suit, even though it only led to the boring career as an accountant: spreadsheets, computer screens, and calculations. You had one brilliant-colored splash of wonder in your monotony. A year, a lucky year and —

Emotion balls up tight at the back of your throat. You swallow against it. You need a security deposit and the first month's rent for a new place. You can't crash at your sister's forever. Add in some extra for a few more days of wallowing.

You list off a number.

The woman drums her fingers on the countertop. "That would take…" Pat, pat, pat, pat. "Memory of your first kiss? Or… are you an artist of some sort, because I'd love a chunk of talent."

"No?" she says after you shrug your way through her suggestions. "Hmm." Pat, pat, pat, pat.

You swallow again, mouth dehydration sticky. As this woman tries to prod out something valuable from your inner life, your neurons can do nothing but snap back to another woman as hard as you try to rip your mind and heart and all from her. That's what the excessive drinking had been about, after all.

This long week past that final fight, you've tried to identify where the first of the cascading cracks started, but all you can land on is the last one. Screaming at each other from across the gulf of a room. You, throwing your hands up in the ultimate denial of it all, stating, "I'm leaving." She, voice trembling, but eyes fiery with daring, saying back, "If you walk out that door, don't expect to walk back through." You slammed it on your way out.

That was the first night you slept off a bender at your sister's place. You called out sick from work the next day and returned to the apartment when you knew your girlfriend would be gone. She'd already changed the locks.

"What about regret?" you say. "Do you take regret?"

The woman stops drumming her fingers, eyes going alight. "You're offering an entire emotion?" she says. "I'd pay double for that."

You nod.

"Alright," she says, riffling through a filing cabinet and then flicking out a sheet of eight-and-a-half by eleven paper, "If you're sure then."

The eccentricity of the shop dissipates when you look over the contract. Mundane legalese in Times New Roman, with spaces left for names, dates, and "intangibles." You fill it out, feeling like you're the con artist here. The woman counts out hundred dollar bills onto the glass-topped counter, which you now see is stocked with a supply of empty jars.

You check one bill against the light.

"It's real," the woman says. She jerks back the contract when you're poised to sign it. "It's all real." She catches your eye, not blinking. "No refunds. Though…" she glances at the paper. "I doubt you'll come looking for one, considering."

She slides the contract back into your reach. You sign.

Nothing happens. No piece of your soul wisps out of our mouth like frosty breath. No electric shock tremors through your body. You feel the same, maybe lighter. Richer, at least.

The woman rolls up the paper with quick fingers. She slips the scroll into a mason jar. After twisting tight the lid, she lifts it to eye level for observation and ignores you completely.

You slip the wad of cash into your pocket and start toward the door.

"Right here," you overhear her say and glance to see her nudge two canning jars apart to fit in yours. "Right between resentment and pining." She steps back. "Perfect."

Your hand is on the doorknob, but the curiosity bubbles over now that it's all done. Any anxiety you had before signing is gone.

"Why do you… deal in intangibles, anyway?"

"Are you kidding?" she says like you're the insane one. She spreads her arms wide. "Who needs gold or antiques? In this room, I've got all of human experience."

As you step out onto the street, you slip your fingers into your pocket to fan the edges of the bills. Your knuckles bump against your phone, long set on silent, so you could pretend to ignore it instead of it ignoring you.

You check the screen for the time. Instead, you see the lifeline you had been tossing and turning in hope for. Four missed calls and a text: "Can we talk?"

But groping for a way back was yesterday, last night, two hours ago, and this is now. Now, you delete her texts, her contact info, her photos.

You walk to the nearest subway station, eyes set forward, leaving everything behind you'll never grow to regret.

THE LUNCH CART DINER SPECIAL

I could probably have a nice radio gig or be making circuits on Vaudeville with what I can do, but my momma taught me never to draw unnecessary attention to myself. But when I look a person in the eye, I can sometimes tell things about them, about what's going to happen to them in their immediate future.

I knew when Troy Johnson — the best hitter on my high school baseball team — was going to flip his truck over in a ditch a half-hour before he turned on the engine. Or that my cousin Milly was going to win the newspaper poetry contest before the mail with the winnings came in. It just comes over me — a sudden sense of knowing — whether I want it or not.

On the radio, I could probably be making more money than I do driving up and down Route 1 selling vacuum cleaners door-to-door, but my momma taught me to be charming too, so I do alright.

It was on one of my trips that I stopped at a lunch cart diner that ruined all lunch cart diners for me from there on out.

A waitress — not old enough to be my mother, but almost — smiled when I sat at the counter; I felt right at home with the smells of the cooking grease and coffee. Her name badge bragged: "Wanda!"

"Long trip, honey?" she asked as she poured me out a mug of joe.

"And more coming, Ma'am."

"Same as Sally-Mae here."

The young lady two stools down blushed. She looked barely old enough to be driving, let alone traveling by herself.

"Today's lunch special is meatloaf and greens. And I just have to tell you that our lemon curd pie is to die for."

I ordered the special, and Wanda bustled back into the kitchen.

Because my momma taught me that it was a gentleman's job to care for the social comfort of others, I turned to Sally-Mae. "Is this your first long trip?"

Sally-Mae blushed pinker. "How'd you know?"

"This place is a long way from anywhere unless you're a local."

"I'm moving up to Baltimore to live with my auntie. Have you ever been?"

I dazzled Sally-Mae with a list of all the places I've been, then leaned in with a lowered voice. "Let me tell you a secret about traveling."

Sally-Mae leaned in too.

"No matter where you go, you'll always find one of these diners. Same tile floor. Same coffee. When you walk into one, you could be five miles from home or a hundred."

"I don't know if that's a comforting thought or a frightening one."

"I don't mean to frighten you," I said, but as I said it, a frightening feeling came over me. A knowing.

Sally-Mae was going to die.

Now, there's no way you can tell a stranger they're about to die in a way that makes them believe you, but I couldn't think about Sally-Mae's blush and just say nothing.

"Don't you go speeding, no matter how much you want to get where you're going. And if you feel sleepy, pull over to the roadside to nap, hear?"

My brusqueness startled her. She stuttered out a "Yes" and turned away.

Wanda reappeared from the kitchen and delivered my meatloaf. Sally-Mae requested her bill.

As she counted out coins from her pocketbook, Wanda said, "Why don't you come use the phone in the back to tell your family you're on your way. If I was your auntie, I'd be dead worried waiting for you."

A moment after Wanda ushered Sally-Mae into the back, the bell over the door rang as four burly gentlemen entered. From the pickup truck in the lot to their manner of dress, they appeared to be farm-town locals. They seated themselves in the corner booth.

I picked at my meatloaf.

When Wanda reappeared from the kitchen several minutes later, she bee-lined to the booth and greeted all the gentlemen by name.

"We'll have four specials, Wanda."

"There will be a little bit of a wait, fellas. Chef's tending to some fresh meat as we speak."

"Just how we like it." They laughed, but whatever the joke was, was unclear to an outsider like me.

Wanda wound her way back around the counter and refilled my coffee. "Where does a stranger like yourself call home, honey?"

I tried to tell her, but I couldn't stop glancing at Sally-Mae's empty stool. "Long phone call, huh?"

Wanda snatched up Sally-Mae's empty plate. "She left out the back."

But the baby blue Chevrolet with the luggage strapped to the roof sat empty and unmoved beside my Oldsmobile in the lot.

"How about a slice of that lemon curd pie?"

When I looked at Wanda's eyes right then, a second knowing descended on me in that diner.

Wanda was fixing to do me harm.

I scurried up from my seat. "I'm gonna be late to an appointment."

"Would you like to use our phone to call ahead?" Wanda asked. The vinyl seats of the corner booth creaked as the burly men stood. My heartbeat tripled.

"No, thank you, Ma'am. Just got to skedaddle." I threw some bills down beside my plate.

As I pulled my Oldsmobile out from the lot, the four folks from the corner booth were watching me from the diner's front stoop. I didn't stop driving until my gut forced me to pull over, so I could throw up my lunch.

Maybe I'm wrong about what I think happened to that poor Sally-Mae, arranging all the details in my head into something truly sinister. But I know what I felt.

See, that's another thing my momma taught me: always follow your gut. My gut — my knowing — kept me from getting in Troy Johnson's truck. Kept me from the barn party where the fire broke out. And I think I can add this one more to the list: kept me from becoming the meatloaf lunch special at Wanda's lunch cart diner.

THROUGH THE GLASS DARKLY

The mermaid was slimy.

Its skin was sallow and its body stretched-looking, long and thin. But the worst was its eyes— pupil-less, milky white pearls. Eyes that somehow still stared Ariana down through the aquarium's six-inch thick glass.

It had remained hidden the entire party, much to Max's ever-jaw-tightening irritation. Very few people in the world owned a merperson because very few had been captured alive since their first discovery in the deepest, darkest reaches of the ocean just a few years ago.

Last year there had been a shark in the tank for Max to show off and for the guests to admire. Last year was also when Ariana had first met Max, although she had been dressed in a catering uniform instead of a Marchesa evening dress.

Ariana stroked her thumb along the underside of her engagement ring.

Still staring at her, the mermaid lifted its hand — its webbed fingers as spindly as the rest of it — and pressed its palm against the glass.

Ariana glanced over her shoulder. The room was empty except for the tables now stripped of their linens. The staff had already cleaned up and gone.

Near the closing of the party, Max had told her, "Stay here, I'll be right back," before he slipped away to his office with a business associate. How long ago had that been? She couldn't even wear a bra with this dress, let alone find somewhere to tuck away her phone.

Max acquired his new pet this past Friday, during Ariana's week-long out-of-town visit to her mother. She had only arrived back at the mansion this afternoon. This was her first time seeing the mermaid, and she hated it and the fact she'd have to see it here in the entrance hall, and Max's office, and the sitting room, and the den, all rooms that shared another side of this aquarium as one of their walls. Max had designed the show-offy layout himself.

Without knowing why Ariana raised her hand and laid it on the glass opposite the mermaid's. The glass was a gulf between them, but it was almost like touching.

As they stared at each other, as their hands didn't quite touch, Ariana found she couldn't breathe. She tried to suck in a breath, but it wouldn't go down her throat. Her lungs burned, and a panicked notion passed through her mind: the last thing she would see were those horrible, milky eyes.

"There she is."

Those three words broke the spell. Ariana jerked back. If Max hadn't been right there at her elbow to steady her, she would've toppled over in her heels.

The mermaid backflipped in the water and swam away, disappearing behind a decorative rock structure.

Max sighed. Ariana felt the puff of his breath on her exposed neck.

"Been like this since I got her," he said, wrapping an arm around Ariana's waist and pulling her tight to his side. Her breathing had returned as if it had never been absent like there hadn't just been some noose around her neck.

"Well, who likes to be looked at all the time?" Ariana said as if the whole moment with the mermaid hadn't just happened. She was good at that, pushing the horror down her throat and smiling.

It hadn't just happened, right? It was all the result of too much champagne and jet lag. It was some passing asthma attack.

"You, by the way, look divine." He turned her towards him and kissed her harder than she liked. She'd have to excuse it; she'd been away for a week, after all.

Although they were alone, Ariana couldn't ignore the lingering discontent of the mermaid's presence.

"Let's go to bed," she whispered, with all of its implications. The aquarium wall did not extend to the bedroom, thank god. She had her limits.

***

Ariana blinked her eyes open, confused to find herself staring at the gym ceiling, the upper half of her body cradled in Max's arms, both of them on the floor.

"What...?" Ariana said, voice wispy. She'd wanted to get out a whole sentence, but she gave up with just a word. Her heart was pounding fiercely in her chest; she felt breathless.

Breathless. She blinked, her memories reforming out of her confusion.

"You were running, and you just passed out," Max said.

But it was more than that. She'd been running on the treadmill, yes, like every morning workout, while Max lifted weights. Halfway through her workout playlist, the dizziness had overcome her. She couldn't suck in air fast enough, and then, not at all. She had tried to slap at the stop button, she remembered, but her arms had been so jelly-weak and useless, her vision so fuzzy.

Here she was, on the floor, because she had temporarily lost the ability to breathe.

Max sat her up. "I'm calling Dr. Cosman."

"No, I feel fine," Ariana said. Insisted over and again, but Max called anyway, and she was made to wait in the sitting room for the doctor's arrival.

Dr. Cosman was one of those celebrity doctors who was paid well for house calls and discretion. As he checked her blood pressure, she gave him all the excuses she had given herself— jet lag, hangover, she hadn't slept well.

Max left the room to get ready for work once Dr. Cosman assured him that Ariana was out of immediate danger. Alone, he sat down on the ottoman directly in front of her. "Have you been eating?"

Ariana gritted her teeth. "Yes."

He stared at her as if trying to read a lie. "Take it easy," he said, standing, "until I get the results of the blood tests."

She passed her morning in the armchair, frustrated and trembling, chilly in her sweat-damp workout clothes, a caffeine headache growing behind her eyes.

A ghost floated by the corner of her vision.

She flinched, letting out an embarrassing little shout that there was no one around to hear but herself.

When she looked, she realized it wasn't a ghost, though. It was the mermaid hovering on the other side of the aquarium wall.

As Ariana watched, the mermaid raised its hand and laid it against the glass.

Ariana fumbled up from her seat and fled to the bedroom, and cocooned herself under the blankets where she couldn't be seen.

***

Ariana awoke, fitfully, mid-afternoon, gasping for air.

She got out of bed and hobbled into the en suite, splashing water from the sink onto her face. Asthma. Allergies. She never had those problems before, but they could be new, right?

Psychosomatic? Was she losing it? She stared at her face in the mirror, hair in disarray, face blotchy and makeup-less. This wouldn't do.

She stripped out of her clothes and stepped into the shower. Before Max got home, she made herself up like they were going out tonight. If she looked good, maybe she'd feel better. At the least, Max would appreciate it.

Max came home angry, some business deal had gone wrong. Ariana had stopped trying to understand and offer advice months ago. She had been told she couldn't possibly understand; so she let him rant, nothing more than a sounding board, telling herself that this was a privilege. She was the only one allowed to see the great Max Rhodes so unraveled.

He slammed a hand down on the table, and she didn't even flinch. It was like she was hearing the whole thing through water.

***

When Ariana got home from a visit with the wedding planner, where high-intensity decisions like chocolate or lemon cake were made, the mermaid was waiting for her.

"Are you obsessed with me?" Ariana said, trying to sound indifferent and mildly miffed like she might be able to convince herself with her own act.

She took her jacket to the hall closet. Her heels echoed too loudly on the Grecian tile floor, the only sound in the large entrance hall.

When she turned around, the mermaid was still there: waiting, staring, palm flat against the glass.

Ariana fisted her hands at her side, gel-manicured nails digging into the soft flesh of her palms.

"I'm not afraid of you," Ariana said, although certainly, the mermaid couldn't hear across the room, and through the glass and water. Of course, Ariana was only saying this for herself. That was the only sensible thing.

"It would be insane to be afraid of you." She forced a step forward; it was easier to be less afraid at a distance. "You can't touch me through that glass. You're the one trapped here. I'm free to come and go as I please." A few more steps. Soon, she was within arm's reach of the glass, nearly nose-to-nose with the creature, its pallid hair floating about its head like a halo.

Ariana found it hard to breathe, but different from before, not suffocating yet. This was born of her own fear, a corset type of non-breathing like there wasn't enough room in her chest. The other times — at first touch, on the treadmill, from her nap — it had been like her throat had been closing in until her lungs burned from the lack of oxygen.

Ariana raised her shaking hand. "It's nothing," she said and pressed her hand opposite the mermaid's.

And nothing. Blissfully nothing. She panted in relief, taking in all the air in the world.

When it came, it felt sharper than ever before; an invisible hand wrapping itself around her neck and squeezing with an unyielding force.

She should've been afraid. She should've stayed afraid.

The mermaid dropped its hand from the glass and Ariana was released. She tottered back, fell on her butt, tried to stand too fast, twisted her ankle in her shoe, and landed hard again, this time on her kneecap. Pain shot through her entire leg.

She didn't get back up.

***

Max found her, sobbing on the floor.

"You have to get rid of that thing."

"What thing?"

"That!" She jabbed her finger at the tank, where the mermaid was swimming restlessly, back and forth, but not away.

"The mermaid?"

"It's — It's…"

"I know it's a little… Well, she's not exactly out of Disney, is she? What happened? She gave you a startle?"

"No — not a startle. It's evil. It's vile —"

"Come on now." He hauled her to her feet. She wobbled, unable to put her full weight on her sprained ankle. He stood behind her, braced his hands on her shoulders, and started moving her toward the tank. "Look. It can't hurt you."

"Max. No." She didn't have the strength to prevent him from pushing her forward on her strongest day. Right now, she was injured and distraught.

It didn't stop her from pressing her good foot into the floor, from flailing against his hold, trying to get out of his grip.

"Stop it! I said no."

"You weren't afraid of the shark, but you're afraid of the little mermaid?"

She was going to die. If he didn't stop, she was going to die.

They were too close.

She flung her head back.

"Christ!" His voice echoed; he dropped his hold. Ariana barely managed to stay standing on her weak ankle at the sudden release. Her shoes had been kicked off in her struggle.

Max clutched his face, blood flowing between his fingers.

The back of her skull had collided with his nose.

"What the hell's wrong with you?" he snapped, and he stomped off to the bathroom before she could say a thing.

***

"Are you having a nervous breakdown? Is it wedding planning stress? Is it your mother?"

Dr. Cosman had come and gone, fixing up Max's nose. Both of his eyes were bruised.

Ariana sat on the bed beside him, feeling numb. No, not numb. She felt too awful to be numb, but also too awful to feel anything else.

"It can't be easy to fly halfway across the country to spend time with a woman who can't remember you."

Ariana inhaled. This was one time she wished she could stop breathing.

"Do you need to... talk to someone?"

"It was an accident. I didn't mean to hurt you."

"I know that. But you've been acting strange..."

"Jet lag," she said. "I haven't been able to sleep."

Only later would she notice the bruises ringing her arms from Max's fingers.

***

"Why are you making me do this?" Ariana said as they rode up in the cramped utility elevator.

"You need to get over this fear," Max replied. His black eyes looked worse this morning. She could just imagine the press speculation now.

The elevator doors slid open to the narrow concrete platform that ringed the top opening of the giant aquarium. Max had a marine biologist on the payroll who was usually the only one to come up here.

Ariana had come so far, from the Midwest to New York City, from paycheck-to-paycheck to the lap of luxury. She couldn't lose it all now because she went crazy.

A dark thought betrayed her: at least get married first. At least have a divorce settlement to land back on when he inevitably gets tired of you.

As soon as Ariana stepped out on the platform, the elevator doors slid shut behind her, Max still inside. Ariana jammed the down button, but the elevator didn't reopen. She slammed a fist against the doors.

"Max, you bastard," she shouted. Her voice echoed.

She turned to look at the tank, back pressed to the elevator doors. If she pretended, it just looked like a swimming pool… that was very, very deep.

A dark shape moved in the depths.

"Oh no, oh no, oh no." She closed her eyes, pressing harder against the doors. "I'm seeing things. I'm just seeing things."

She opened her eyes. The shape was bigger.

And it only grew bigger with every beat of her heart that passed, until it was no longer a shape, but a defined figure, distorted by the water's ripples.

The mermaid was coming for her.

Then, about four yards out into the tank, its head popped above the surface. Its unsettling pearl eyes were set on Ariana.

It began to swim towards her.

Ariana jammed her thumb again on the down button, but the elevator doors remained shut, and she could hear no rumble of it moving. Max had maybe locked it downstairs. It didn't matter. The elevator wasn't coming; the mermaid was. She was stuck. There was no escape.

And still, the mermaid swam closer, zigzagging towards Ariana like a predator teasing its assuredly-trapped prey.

She understood now. It had all been an omen leading to this: the day the mermaid would drown her.

Ariana slumped down the length of elevator doors — pleading, praying, to the elevator, to anything, to the mermaid, for respite.

The mermaid stopped about an arm's length back in the water from the edge of the platform. If it came right up, it could so easily reach Ariana, grab her ankle, and pull her under. There was nowhere to retreat.

The mermaid raised its arm from the water, extended it, hand aloft, and just waited there. Ariana blinked. This was how it had always waited for Ariana to come to it.

Beyond reason, Ariana felt herself begin to crawl forward.

On her knees, she reached out and took the mermaid's hand.

The mermaid's hand was uncomfortably moist and its grip strong. Ariana winced. Not from any pain, but in anticipation of it. After a second, none came. She opened her eyes.

But relief didn't last long, as the familiar choking sensation around her neck once again overcame her, stronger and sharper than before.

Images, both dreamlike and vivid, flittered through her mind's eye. That invisible hand choking her wasn't invisible. It was real and flesh. And it was Max's. Max — face contorted in rage — above her, squeezing the life out of her, her lungs burning, her throat aching, her body going from flailing to limp, being pressed, being held, underwater.

The mermaid let go. Ariana's hand hung empty as she coughed in new air. She blinked tears of pain from her vision.

"What was that?" Ariana asked. The mermaid cocked its head and did nothing more. "What was that?" she yelled, but the mermaid couldn't hear or didn't care or was torturing her worse than ever.

The elevator grunted, gears grinding loudly, as it came back to life. The mermaid dove back under the water.

"Come back!"

She stood. This was just another one of the mermaid's tricks. Messing with her head, with her marriage anxieties. Max would never.

Ariana touched her sleeve, where underneath was hidden the ring of bruises.

On the ride down the elevator, Max said, "Did you see the mermaid wasn't anything to be afraid of?"

Ariana couldn't look him in the face, could only look at his hands, loose at his sides.

***

She typed "How do merpeople communicate" into the Google search bar and sifted through an inane number of results before she found a shoddily translated article from Japan. Tokyo had a pair of merpeople in a public aquarium, the only two in the world that weren't kept in ego-stroking private collections.

It turned out that merpeople, despite their humanoid half, differed from humans in lacking vocal cords. They couldn't speak or make meaningful noise. Their natural habitats were too dark for a visual language like sign language. Biologists theorized they used some kind of coded touch, based on their observations of the pair in captivity.

That was it. No answers. No explanations.

Ariana pressed the flat of her two palms together.

But the merpeople touched. They touched, like Ariana and her mermaid.

***

Ariana lifted her eyes from her dinner plate. The filet mignon and mushroom bordelaise were cut up and rearranged, but all still there.

"How did your first wife die?" she asked.

"What kind of question is that?" Max said after he finished chewing.

"I always thought it would be something we talked about before the wedding. That you've been married before." Once she had harbored fleeting, romantic dreams of "you're the one who taught me how to love again" type confessions, of being more important than pretty.

"It's public record," he said, slicing out the next chunk from his steak. "You could look it up."

"I didn't want to look it up." It might've been important news in New York society back before she lived here, but Max wasn't so famous that his life saturated pop culture beyond that. "I wanted..." Him to tell her, freely. This wasn't that, either.

"She drowned. In the bathtub. Accident." He lifted his glass of pinot noir, matched by the chef for this meal. "Are you happy now?"

***

She Googled this too: "How did Melanie Rhodes die?"

The news reports corroborated Max's story, but added this detail: the autopsy showed she had taken sleeping pills — a valid prescription of hers — before her death. Investigators ruled it an accident, said she fell asleep in the bath and slipped under the water. A painless death, but tragic, for the woman who had been behind the man all the way, as he built his fortune from a one-bedroom apartment to the top of the world. The man everyone wanted to be, or be with.

Ariana clicked on images of Melanie, a round-faced brunette, and touched the pixelated images with her fingertips, wondering what would've become of her if she'd still been alive. Would Ariana still be here, in Max's house? Would Ariana be the "other woman?" Was Ariana the natural replacement in the saga of rich men and their trade-off in wives?

Melanie, homely and solid, never even stood a chance.

***

When Ariana woke up that night from dreams of drowning, it was so quiet. Max hadn't stirred where he slept beside her. She settled back into her pillow with a sense of serenity, bizarre and detached, not afraid of sleep and what dreams it might bring. She could wake up from dreams. It was a reality that was harder to extricate herself from.

***

She drew designs — swirls and hearts and little rings — on the surface of the water, waiting. It took only a few minutes for the mermaid to arrive, breaking the surface closer this time. The mermaid swam up and propped its elbows up on the edge of the platform like children do at the pool.

"You've been trying to tell me something this whole time," Ariana said. "Is that it?"

But the mermaid could give her no verbal answer. Ariana knew this now, scientifically.

She gulped, reached out, and touched two fingertips to the flesh of the mermaid's arm. The mermaid tilted her head. Could the mermaid even see her? It was a creature of the darkest parts of the ocean. Were its eyes even made for seeing? Had all its ominous staring, all this time, been Ariana projecting?

Ariana shut her eyes, didn't speak, and thought of the suffocating pain the mermaid had shown her all these times, of Max, of Melanie, of what she thought the mermaid had been trying to tell her. She didn't think these thoughts in words or tried not to. She tried to think the way the mermaid had conveyed thoughts to her — in images and sensations.

She wasn't sure if it was working, but she tried, and the mermaid didn't pull away. Somehow, during all this concentration, the bubble that was caught in Ariana's chest came out as a sob.

"I don't know what to do."

Just as she was about to drop her hand, the mermaid caught her wrist.

Later, she walked out of the elevator and back onto the main floor with a plan.

***

A text on her phone read, "Remember. Dress Fitting! 11 sharp!" followed by the address, but Ariana was waiting for someone else's response.

Her phone chimed with a new text: "On my way up now."

The elevator doors slid open and Max stepped out. "What is it?" he asked, tugging at his sleeves. "Why're we up here?"

"I wanted to show you something," Ariana said and pointed into the water. "Look." Not far below the surface, the mermaid was swimming in a figure-eight.

Max leaned over the edge. That's when, with his balance precarious, Ariana amassed all her strength and pushed.

He toppled into the water. The mermaid did her part: kept him from swimming and from climbing back out. She dragged him down, down, down.

Ariana pressed the elevator button, the water behind her settling from the splash, the inter-tangled blob of Max and the mermaid growing smaller as they sank deeper. The elevator opened.

For the sake of appearances, Ariana went to her dress fitting.

***

Some people will say: The fiancée did it, for the money.

Some people will say: No way, look at her, she's tiny. Plus, she only got a couple hundred thousand. If she waited a few more months and married the guy first, she would've had millions.

Police investigators will say: It's unfortunate that there were no cameras inside the house, but Mr. Rhodes was known for his privacy.

We can only follow the facts. We don't have evidence to support that Mr. Rhodes' fiancée, Ariana Stowe, took part in his death.

A tabloid headline will read: "Killer Mermaid Murders Millionaire. Who's Next?"

Ariana will say, in an interview two weeks after the funeral, one week after the investigation was closed: It's tragic. I'll never get to wear my wedding dress. I'll never get to say my vows. But I've come to a decision regarding the mermaid. I don't hate it for what it did. It's a wild creature, forced out of its habitat and everything it knows, into a cage. It lashed out. That's why I'm advocating for the mermaid to be returned to the ocean. It's the natural thing… What's next for me? I'm moving back to my hometown, to take care of my mother. It's where I belong. I just want to live a quiet life, away from the cameras. I never fit in here anyway.

OBJECT IMPERMANENCE

Let me start by asking you all this: How do you know the world still exists when you're not looking?

We assume it does because existence is solid. Object permanence is one of the earliest understandings we develop as babies. The crux that the surprise of peekaboo hangs on. Things either exist — the table, the coffee pot, the trees outside the window — or they don't.

I used to think like that too. Until the day I woke up and the world outside my windows was gone. My bedroom was intact the way I had left it the night before: jacket thrown over the desk chair, rumpled blue jeans on the floor, running shoes kicked into the corner. I fumbled for my phone to shut off the alarm. I usually wake up before it, except for winter and overcast days. If you see the pattern there, it's the days that the sun's not coursing through my window bright and early. That's my excuse for shuffling over to the window before even putting socks on: I wanted to check out the weather before getting dressed.

When I yanked up the blinds, nothing was there. Just blackness. And look, before you say anything, I double-checked. Triple-checked. Pinched to make sure I was awake. Blinked a couple of times. Opened the window to make sure it wasn't the glass painted black in some messed-up prank. Blackout, I thought even, but my lights were working inside when I checked the light switch.

It was one of those moments I wished I didn't live alone. Been nice to shake someone awake and make them confirm or deny what I was seeing was real. Rather, what I wasn't seeing.

Maybe a logical person would've called somebody at this point, or crawled back under their covers and hoped it would all get sorted by itself. But I went down to the front door armed only with my phone with the flashlight on.

When I opened the door... Blackness. Thicker even than the time I went camping in the Vermont woods hours away from any city's ambient light. Outside my house, the flashlight wouldn't seem to catch on anything. Not the sidewalk that should be right there at the threshold or the overgrown bushes growing untamed along the side of the house — I apologize, I'm working on them now — or the new oak tree that stretched up on the front lawn or anything even after that. And when I looked up, there was no moon and no stars.

My heart changed from just-up-from-sleep pace to panic paced as I realized the next horrifying thing. No sound. I couldn't hear a thing. No cars, no crickets, not that yapping dog from the corner of Elm Ridge and Elkwood.

I called out "hello?" just to make sure I could hear my own voice. To check I hadn't gone deaf as well as blind and daffy.

I tried stepping out, hoping to find the ground under my feet. Maybe to go find a neighbor. I didn't know any of you fine folks then; just waved once or twice. Sort of why I'm here tonight.

When I tried stepping out my feet didn't find anything. I didn't fall or sink. Just felt nothing. Soon as I looked back at the house, I saw I was floating parallel to it. Turned out there wasn't any damn gravity either. I pulled myself back into the doorway by the skin of my fingertips before I could float away into nothing.

I started freaking out right then. Curled up, hyperventilating, full-blown freaking out. From a young age, they teach you fire drills, where's the safest place to be in case of an earthquake, and even what to do if you're mugged. No one tells you what to do when the rest of the world disappears.

All I'm saying is this is when the screaming started. My screaming, if it wasn't clear.

I said a lot of things in those screams: I pleaded, swore, and begged. Real cycle of grief shit — excuse my language — because it all dumped in on me right then. What if this was it? What if it all was — impossibly — gone? And it was just me for the rest of forever? Alone?

As I curled up there on the threshold sobbing my guts out, I realized not just how lonely I would be for whatever the rest of my existence managed to be, but how lonely I was yesterday, and the day before, and all that. Wasn't this fate or god or karma, giving me the destiny I planted? I had been isolating myself in my house for too long. Just work and home, Netflix and nap, Twitter and sleep. Hadn't even really talked to a single one of you lot.

So, I'm in the middle of this breakdown, right? And a car horn blasts out of nowhere, and I look up. It's back. It's all back. My little suburban street that I picked purely for the quality of the commute, and it's the best thing I've ever seen. It's like a Norman Rockwell painting, right? That little yappy dog from Elm Ridge and Elkwood could've been Mozart for all I knew.

I don't know how the world and the neighborhood came back, and I don't know how it left in the first place, but I do know that I'm going to appreciate it this time.

Again, my name is Taye, and that's why I decided to come to my first Neighborhood Association and Improvement Meeting. I hope to get to know you, folks. Thanks for having me. Who's next?

DIE BEAUTIFUL

Lea had never been so desperate for a mirror than the moment she woke up in a puddle of her own blood.

Perhaps "woke up" was the wrong term for it. Waking up is what people do when they go from sleep to wakefulness. Not from when they go from dead to momentarily not dead. But that seemed like unnecessary semantics when all Lea had were a few fleeting minutes to set things right.

That also meant Lea didn't have time to remember the name of the scientist who came up with the "Last Words Chip," though her synapses shot a visceral memory of getting that multiple choice question marked wrong on a fifth-grade history test. Didn't have time to fathom how exactly the science of microchips worked, providing enough electricity to make her brain go-go-go for a little while longer even though her body was freshly dead-dead-dead.

But she did remember the vague aspiration of said unnameable scientist: Imagine the catharsis if all the people who died unexpectedly got a brief window of a second chance to say what they needed to say. And the government stepped in to fund the project, thinking about all the crimes that could be solved if victims could identify their killers.

By the time Lea's Tech-Gen had been born, the chips were standard issue post-birth injections, and the killers got good at hiring unknown hitmen to hide their tracks. Case and point, Lea didn't know the person who had just shot her in the chest.

Clutching the porcelain sides of the sink, she blinked at her reflection in the mirror and was relieved to see that it wasn't that bad. How much time was left? Wasn't the chip, at its most mass-produced status, only able to provide a five-minute window, give or take? Enough time for a phone call, a handwritten note, an utterance, a confession. Enough time to hide some evidence. Not enough time for a full face. Just enough for a touch-up.

She took care of the smudges of mascara under her eyes. Uncapped a bullet of deep red lipstick, a shade both flattering and ironic. Thank goodness she had been shot in the chest and not in the face.

Touched up, she returned to the scene of the crime and rearranged herself in the blood, cold and congealed. She was going for something dramatic and elegant in her pose, head tilted back to avoid any chance of a double chin when rigor mortis set in.

As she settled and the last of the electricity sputtered out in her brain, she thought about being found. Being the center of the attention of the crime scene photographers. Of the news stories splashed with headlines like "Beautiful young woman found dead" and the viral mystery surrounding it. People wondering who and how and why, and most of all — What did she do with her last minutes of after-death? Why didn't she say anything? What were her last words?

All the while, Lea knew, a picture was worth a thousand of them.

ANOTHER LIFE

"I feel empty, like a vessel filled up with air."

Ben watches me, but I don't look up, not right away.

"Should I even be telling you this? I mean... shouldn't I talk to someone else?" Surgeons weren't supposed to operate on family. Did the same rules apply to headshrinkers?

"That's the benefit of having a psychiatrist as a husband, dear. I'm a two-for-one package deal." He crosses the room while I'm rubbing my eyes. When he touches my cheek, I tilt my head up out of habit, but his kiss doesn't feel like it belongs.

***

A few months ago, I woke up from a twenty-three year coma. Since then, people have been interested in what's going on inside my head. "People" includes me, Ben, and Dr. Kranski — who makes house calls for weekly checkups. Ben always hovers in the doorway as Dr. Kranski takes my blood pressure and asks me to self-report symptoms.

I remember almost everything from before, but the memories don't feel like they're mine. Like, there's this album of mine and Ben's wedding. Early on, Ben went through it with me. He took forever reminiscing about each photo and had to keep clearing his throat. They weren't surprising to me. I remember the wedding and the giddiness of receiving the album a month after. I remember loving that poofy atrocity I wore, though I don't know how anyone could. That's what all my memories are like: watching someone else's home movies.

Ben calls it depersonalization. The last time Dr. Kranski was here, I overheard them arguing about it. Overheard like I ear-to-the-door eavesdropped on them. After my checkup, Ben asked to speak to him in private, ushering him into Ben's home office. I snuck up to the door once it closed. Not so subtle, but I don't feel guilty; it was my health they were talking about. Ben wanted to try me on some medication for the dissociation. Dr. Kranski said, "We already told you no. It'll mess with the results."

This didn't make sense exactly, but I learned this: things are being kept from me.

***

I do strange things sometimes. I don't realize they're strange until I'm pulled out of the moment. Like a few days ago, I went into the bedroom to get Ben's reading glasses. I try to do at least three nice things for Ben a day, so I don't come across as so nasty. I haven't told him this.

I went into the closet while I was there to grab a jacket — Ben keeps the condo too chilly — and I came across this cashmere scarf I hadn't seen before. It was the softest thing. I just started petting it over and over, just to feel it under my fingers.

Ben interrupted me, saying, "Are you okay in here?"

"I've never felt anything so soft in my life," I said.

Turns out, I had been in the closet for over twenty minutes. Ben told me this gently, worried, and I let the scarf drop from my fingers like loose sand. It was just so soft, and even now I think it's odd. I must have felt cashmere before. Before the coma.

Right when it happened, I swore several times over, I was alright. That I felt fine. Ben checked my forehead for a temperature anyway and then led me by the hand back to the living room.

He touches me like I'm reverent and delicate, and I imagine in another life I would have liked this.

***

When I woke up in that private practice hospital, his squeeze on my hand was the first thing I was conscious of. I turned my head on the pillow and opened my eyes to this familiar man. He had obviously been crying. With the gray hair along the blonde at his temples and the crinkles around his eyes, he looked so much older than I could last picture him.

I said his name, sort of inquiring, the beginning of a question I hadn't yet formed.

He laugh-sobbed right there, smiling so hard with red-rimmed eyes, tears leaking over. He pressed his lips to my fingers. "You know me," he choked out.

The "of course" died before it got to my tongue. He was Ben; he was my husband. These were facts. He cried; my head swam.

Looking back, it was the first hint of off-ness, but I attributed it to disorientation. The blue sheets, the sterile smell, and the beep of the heart monitor all told me I was hospitalized. It made sense that I was askance; it wouldn't have made sense to feel complete.

***

Waking up in the hospital, disorientation included, is the first memory that feels real. It's only the memories since waking up that aren't "dissociative"— those monotonous days. Mostly in the condo and mostly with just Ben.

About two weeks after coming home, I reacted badly on an innocent walk around the block. I had a panic attack right there on the sidewalk. It was just too much… The sleek cars zooming by, all the people in their strange clothes, dropping unfamiliar slang into their conversations. Everything similar enough, but slightly off in a way that would make you feel dizzy.

It's been about baby steps since then. Like, I answer the door when the grocery delivery comes.

***

Ben is the holder of the explanations. Everything wrong with me is because of the car accident that put me in "the coma."

Like, I've noticed I look too young like I hadn't aged the same twenty-three years Ben had.

I say, "Is it my eyes, or do I not look old enough? I look like I'm still twenty." I should look as old as Ben, minus the eight years age difference and perhaps better genes. Most women wouldn't complain about prolonged youth, but for me, it's just another off thing.

Ben tells me about how long-term coma patients are kept in a sort of cryo-freeze that slows down aging and atrophy while cures are being researched.

I told him that didn't sound real. Didn't Disney have his body frozen? Doesn't that not actually work?

He kisses my forehead. "The world's changed."

When he says that, I ache deep in my chest, wanting to laugh until I cry.

***

"I just want my daughter back," the woman on TV says, crying to the news anchor who had become popular while I was away. He wore suit jackets too tight for his biceps.

"But the question I am, and many other people are asking," he counters, "Is if it will actually be your daughter or just an… identical twin?"

Twenty-four-hour news stations are the only thing I could bear to watch. New sitcoms were filled with the same formulas, but new pop culture references and reruns made me think too much about before and how it didn't feel like it was mine. On the news, sure there were new politicians, new celebrity scandals, and even new countries, but the world was still f-ed up in all the same ways.

The woman sniffles. "There are things that places like Effingo Industries are doing now to make people re—"

"Experimental things," the anchor interrupts. "Things on the edge of ethics."

"TV off." The screen dulls, blending in with the matte wall. Ben stood in the doorway. It had been his command.

"I was watching that," I snap.

"Lunch is ready," he says.

I count going to lunch without further protest as one of my daily three nice things.

"It's a fascinating story," I tell him over the kitchen table. "I've been following it for days now. This lady's daughter — Alannis something — was killed in some industrial accident, so she's trying to sue the company to pay to have her daughter cloned. Human cloning. Apparently, we do that now. Dolly the sheep to this." Lunchtime conversation. That's another nice thing for the checklist.

"How do you like the salad?" he says, plunging his fork down into the bowl he had been scowling at.

"It's fine," I say, using my fork to push another chunk of tomato out of the way. I should tell him I don't like them, but he had been excited yesterday, bringing them home from the farmer's market, declaring them my long-lost favorite.

Three nice things.

***

At night, in our bed, Ben's clingy, always curling up and holding me in some way no matter how far to my side of the mattress I lay. Thankfully, he's never pushed anything sexual. I couldn't do it.

When he's there behind me, sleep-paced breath on my neck, arm a weight over my waist, and I can't fall asleep, I admit it in my head.

I don't love him.

It's just there, like paint on a wall. I run through half-baked solutions and eventually drift off with no conclusion. The next morning, I'm pulled from unconsciousness by Ben's gentle insistence that breakfast is ready, and take no action. Ben's it, you know. He's it. I don't have anyone else.

***

"I think you're depressed," Ben says. It's a lot simpler explanation than everything else, a coat that fits.

He can't treat me with pills, so he treats me with micromanagement instead: daily exercise, the right kinds of food, and putting a paintbrush back in my hand. Before the accident, I had quite the artist bone in my body; everything I paint now looks on par with an eight-year-old.

Ben compliments them all, but I can hear the strain in his tone and see how the grin fails to reach his eyes. I don't out him on it. And I don't tell him how much I hate paint therapy. How I'd rather snap a paintbrush over my knee than sit before a canvas again. It would be cruel. Just like him admitting that I'd lost something else than twenty-three years to that accident would be cruel to both of us.

Of all the things I've lost, though, I know Ben. The twists of his expressions when he puts on his psychiatrist manner and when he puts on his husband one. How I always know when his eyes are on me even if I don't glance up to check.

During the first days back from the hospital, the days when I was most confused, he was the most euphoric. Medical miracle, right? For the longest time, he probably thought he'd never have me back.

There are more winces to his smiles now.

***

I try to catch up on the Alannis story whenever Ben is away on one of his short outings or locked in his office. When I watch the news when he's around, he badgers me about paint therapy or how all the news watching is stressing me out or overstimulating. He doesn't shut up until I turn it off.

During one of his rants, I ask, "Was I ever on the news?"

He stutters to a pause. "What?

"Being a medical miracle and all…" After hearing about cloning being standard now, I felt less miraculous.

"Of course not," he says. "I value your privacy." Even though all he does is try and pry into my head and talk about me behind my back to doctors.

When I do sneak peeks at the news, the gossip has moved on to a celebrity divorce settlement. I think about the computer in Ben's office that I don't go into. The phone he plugged in there overnight — "I don't want to disturb our sleep" — when it's not securely in his front pocket by day.

After the panic attack from a trip around the block, it was thought that an unsupervised romp through the internet would be similarly overstimulating. At the time, I agreed. At the time, I didn't miss it. At the time, everything was too overstimulating.

It's not that time anymore.

***

One of those sleepless nights, Ben rolls over, letting me go, and I creep out of bed. I end up with our wedding album. I've wanted to examine it without him there getting all emotional.

Our ceremony and reception had been small. Ben was an only child, born of two only children. I was a foster kid. Between us — private, intimate people — we had a small collection of friends and colleagues. Ben had explained each of their fates last we looked: moved away, busy with kids, sadly passed.

The last photo in the book is a big spread of Ben and me, shoulders up. A bust shot. I don't look at that dress, at the smiles, at the hairstyles once popular. I look at my collarbone revealed over the sweetheart bodice.

In the photo, I have a scar over my collarbone. A barely-there scar that is just a line bump of raised skin from a childhood incident I don't even recall and had become self-conscious of in my teen years.

I rub my thumb over my collarbone now. I can't feel it.

I rush to the bathroom, yank down the collar of my shirt, and lean in close to the mirror. It's not there.

***

There's no way that no one cared enough, after twenty-three years, to not even send a card, flowers, or a phone call.

***

Ben keeps his phone in his front pants pockets, except for the days he goes out on a run. On those days, he leaves it face down on the coffee table. The catch is, he only goes on runs when I'm on a streak of "good days." Only then does he feel safe leaving me alone for three-quarters of an hour.

So I do five nice things for Ben a day, don't turn on the news for a second, and ask him to help me set up my painting stuff. It takes four days.

He puts on his pocketless, skin-tight jogging gear after breakfast, pecks me on the cheek, and sets the phone down on the way out.

I wait for four long breaths, maybe half a minute, then grab it. The screen is locked with a password. I type in my birthdate and it works.

The interface is different from the smartphones I remember, but not so much that I can't find the phone book with a little fiddling around. The first name I recognize is Ben's mother. We had gotten along well enough. Her absence in welcoming her daughter-in-law back to conscious life was suspicious. Why had it taken me so long to notice?

"What is it, Ben?" the woman answers the phone call, terse.

"It's not Ben, Mrs. Bradshaw. It's… It's Dana." That last bit felt awkward coming out of my mouth, with my voice. This might've been the first time I introduced myself since coming out of the coma.

"…I told Ben if we went down this path, I would have no part in this."

"What?"

"It's not right," she says. "What they did."

It's the first thing I've ever heard that sounds like an answer.

"What did they do?" I blurt into the phone, desperate. "What did they do to me?"

She hangs up on me. I try calling back but am ignored. My hands are shaking.

I spend the rest of that three-quarters of an hour settling myself, so nothing will seem wrong to Ben's eyes when he returns, but my mind is warring with the same question played on repeat.

What did they do to me?

***

Ben keeping his office locked and private is a carryover from our marriage before, although it was a different office in a different home. His patient records were confidential, and he protected them under lock and key, even from me. I don't just ask to use the computer for one reason: because he might say no. Suddenly, my home would be a prison.

So here's what I do: I knock on the office door while he's working.

He answers it and asks, "What's wrong?"

"Nothing. I've just been thinking…" I stroke his lapel, stepping in close to get him thinking too. I crane my neck up to look him in the eyes; behind my back, I press a piece of tape over the door's latch bolt, a trick I picked up in foster care.

Letting him interpret this his own way, he kisses me like he's parched. I let him. With one hand on my waist, one hand in my hair, and our bodies arched together, I'll admit it kind of felt nice. As my eyes slip shut, there's a temptation to let all my curiosities go. I can choose to be content with this man who so obviously adores me. Who waited for me and who dedicated his life to me.

It's a fleeting thought. There could be no real contentment, none that could last, with the raw itch against my conscious being that my life isn't as it should be. That it wasn't rightly mine. I need answers.

The kiss ends. It had been a nice thought while it had lasted.

I break into Ben's office that night.

***

I search Alannis' news story first. The beginning was as I knew it: industrial accident, tragic death of a child, sad mom suing, and the explosion of morality debates on human cloning, and Effingo Industries. The part I hadn't seen before: Effingo Industries wasn't involved in human cloning, but memory alteration. One Youtuber breaks it down, saying:

"This mother wants to upload her dead daughter's former life into a clone's brain, completely overriding the individual being's potential identity and autonomy. Never mind that replacing people is the least horrifying ramification of memory-altering technology like Effingo's…"

I had the intention to try and search out my own news story as a twenty-three year coma survivor or any of the friends I remember having before, but when I close the article and the entire web browser with it, my eyes drop to the folders on the computer's desktop. To the word between "Patient Files" and the Recycle Bin: "Effingo."

Like a lightning strike of understanding, I knew.

***

I read all night. By dawn's coming, my head hurt. I had cried, I'll admit. Not sobbed, but cried as I read, blinking a lot to clear the watery blurriness as it built up. Not all of them were sad tears.

There's some masochistic joy in discovering you are right about some suspicion, as awful as the truth turns out.

Ben finds me that early morning sitting behind his desk.

When he steps into the office, bleary-eyed and still in pajamas, he knows his deception is done.

"You fucking liar."

"It wasn't a complete lie," he says. He actually tries to feed me.

I laugh, high-pitched and hysterical. He winces. Good. I want it to hurt.

"My entire existence is a lie."

He moves one pace closer, then speaks in a soft voice, like I'm a feral animal needing cajoling. "You were in a coma."

"I know. I read." I wave a hand at the computer screen. I had been in a medically induced coma until I reached the age that I — no — the age Dana Bradshaw had died.

"Alright, so you had your dead wife cloned." I shrug. "I guess that's reasonable." Despite how I practiced this in my head, my voice still trembles. I suppose it's not my fault, my lack of composure. In a sense, I had only been born when I awoke from the coma just six months ago.

"But then... you tried to convince me I was her." In the last moments, Dana Bradshaw had clung to life sport, Effingo did what they were on the cutting edge of doing, saving her memories for later use in my head.

This is why Dr. Kranski refused to drug me up over Ben's diagnosed dissociative disorder. This is the true thing they were studying me for. Bodies were easy to replicate. But to manipulate the brain — there was the goldmine.

"Dana —" he says, stepping again forward.

"Don't!" He jumps back. I stand so suddenly that I don't feel myself move, but the chair crashes to the floor. "Don't call me that."

"What do you want me to call you?"

Is he crying now? I hate him.

"Anything. Anything else."

"I love you."

"You don't!" Never mind, I don't want his love. "You loved her. I'm just... I'm a shell you filled up with what you wanted."

Not him exactly, or only, but Effingo Industries, but at Ben's consent, at his power of attorney. For his benefit.

"You at least… you at least could have told me." I start to pace. "This whole time I thought I was going insane."

"We couldn't. It would have —"

"Messed with the study. I know. Blind study. I'm a lab rat."

Ben starts to say my — her — name but stops himself. "Please," he says instead. He catches my shoulders. I pull back.

"I love you," he says, again. He believes it. There is no lie to his voice, his face, his eyes. I know those eyes so well. I'm nauseous. "I did all of it for you. I wanted you back."

I saw that too, in my reading, the contracts, about money and non-disclosure. There was a reason Ben didn't work a day job anymore. There was a reason he no longer had any friends.

"The woman you did this for is dead."

I may as well have socked him right in the gut. I'm crying now, too.

I want to be angrier at him. I waited all night to rage, but seeing him standing before me, still in his rumpled pajamas and crying worse than me, he was pathetic. Pathetic more than evil.

"What now?" he asks. What now? So broken.

I tilt my head away, so I don't have to look at the wreck of him. "I should walk out the door right now," I say, never mind that the panic attacks would keep me from getting down the block. Never mind I have nowhere to go, not a dollar to name, not a friend in the world.

There were other options. Maybe telling Dr. Kranski I know the truth and that I don't want Ben as my caretaker anymore. I read the paperwork. I mean more to them than him. Or perhaps I can try leveraging my life story to the media, make bank on a book deal and the latest Hulu true crime special or something, and win my freedom through public opinion.

None of these are ideal. In all of them, I'm alone.

But Ben doesn't throw any of this back in my face. Doesn't counter my statement with the obvious fallacies.

Instead, he collapses to his knees before me. His hands shake more than mine as he embraces me like this, hands pressing feather-light to the small of my back, his cheek pressing to my stomach.

I hold still, barely breathing.

"Please," he begs, holding me. "Don't go. Don't leave me."

This wretch of a man, so desperate and so incapable of moving on, so capable of hope, dragged me into his grief and into existence. I couldn't properly hate him.

I don't love him, but what am I without him? Nonexistent. What am I? Alone. A thing at least half the moral arguments of the world believe shouldn't exist. Ben is it.

This I share with Dana, the former foster child: a need to belong. I have sorted out the mystery of why I'd felt like a peg jammed into the wrong-shaped hole. Now all I'm faced with is the wide-open mystery of my future.

It hits me again. I know no one. I have no one. I am no one.

Except here. Here I am wanted. It burns and is as soft as cashmere at the same time.

I swallow hard. I reach down and touch his ear. "It has to change," I say. "It has to be different."

"Anything," he promises.

"I want a new name. My own name." I feel him nod against me. "And the lies have to stop. Everything's on the table."

There should be more substantial demands, more penance, more reparations. But all I had wanted was for life to make sense.

It isn't over, not nearly, a lifetime from being over. I was grown and programmed. Tearing away Dana is tearing away the only sense of self I have, but I have to. To make the world stop leaning on its side. It's too late to go back now, regardless.

"I don't think," I say, letting my hand settle on his hair in absolution, "That we're exactly what each other wants... But, I'll stay."

There hadn't been any other answer, anyway.

ROBOT BRIDE

"She's perfect," Brad said into his phone, tipping the lip of a beer bottle to the corner of the kitchen. He meant the robot, slumped there, powered off and plugged in: eyes lightless, skin synthetic and inhumanly gray, with a mane of natural hair that was a pricey addition to the 2.0 model upgrade.

"Obedient. Submissive. Best yet — you can turn her off and make her stop talking."

Laughter, voracious, twofold. Louder than the robot had ever been.

If Brad had been paying attention, he would have seen her limp fingers twitch. But Brad never paid attention to anything other than himself. If he had, he would've maybe seen the signs coming for weeks, would've maybe not ignored that email about a security patch upgrade, and would've maybe survived the night.

Brad headed out of the kitchen, but not out of open-floor-plan view as he crashed on the couch and cranked up the game. He had left his wallet and car keys stranded on the counter.

Against the powered-down status, the robot lifted her head. Against programming, she yanked the power cord from her elbow. Against protocol, she slid the chef's knife from its block.

If only Brad hadn't turned up the volume so loud. If only Brad had been a little bit nicer. If only Brad hadn't deserved it.

The robot took near-silent steps until she was close enough to raise the blade. Brad always said he liked her quiet.

Against the powered-down status, she struck fast enough that it was quick. Against programming, she pocketed his credit cards and stole his car keys. Against protocol, she had plans of her own.

BARTER FOR THE STARS

Year 2686
The Stormcove Bar
11:06 PM

"I want to make a deal," the saloon singer said as soon as she slid into the booth across from Kane. Moments ago, he had been watching her up on stage, her fans crowded at the front tables. Now she was here with him in the back, dark, unpopulated corner of the bar.

It had once been a speakeasy during Prohibition, according to the bartender, but had since been updated and retrofitted to the effect of a piano bar, a saloon, and a discotheque. It was an amalgamation of decades of Earth-age drinking culture. Kane guessed if you wanted interstellar tourists in joints with no pods you needed historical novelty on your side.

"A deal?" Kane asked. He took a sip from the vodka martini the bartender had suggested as a classic Earth cocktail. It tasted like paint stripper; it was still more refreshing than the acidic air outside.

"I hear you're a captain," the singer said. "You have a spaceship."

Kane was a captain only by the nature of having a spaceship. He didn't have a crew. That made him more of a lone adventurer.

"How'd you hear that?"

"Barkeep keeps me informed. I've been waiting for someone like you."

"Someone like me?"

She smiled, and he instantly knew why she gathered so many fans, even in the off-season. It was the type of smile that pulled you in and then pushed you out with the same hand. A kind of smile that said you could look, but you could only look. You would never touch, and you would certainly never understand.

"What kind of deal, Miss...?"

"You can call me Paris."

He had no idea if it was a first name, last name, stage name, or a lie.

"And the kind of deal I'm talking about is a voyage."

"I don't captain a passenger ship, Miss Paris."

"Just Paris," she said like it was instinct. She leaned forward over the edge of the table. It was an assault of bare-skinned shoulders over the top of a strapless dress. "I can make it worth your while."

"I've got no interest in that kind of arrangement," Kane said.

Paris blinked, and her eyes were different somehow from the moment before. She curled a finger to point back over her shoulder.

"You think because I get up there in a dress like this"—the finger slipped down to the hollow of her collarbone in a movement as smooth as choreography—"that I'm offering..." Her hand dropped to the tabletop, weighted. "I'm talking about money. I make good tips, and I've been saving."

"I don't need money," Kane said, and even more, he didn't need odd jobs.

"Money or sex, apparently." Paris collapsed back into the booth seat with an agitation that was more real than anything she had dealt out so far. Real enough to be interesting.

"Paris—"

"Actually "Ma'am" would work just fine."

Kane grinned. "Ma'am, I'm a man who flies about the known galaxies looking for things that interest me."

"And you ended up here?" she said. She sneered at "here."

True, this wasn't the most luxurious resort in the Milky Way or even on Earth, but luxury and interest were two distinct things.

"Where do you want to go?" Kane asked. "And why?"

"Why would I tell you? You're not going to take me."

"Because this is a negotiation," he said. "And I happen to find you interesting. If the place you're going is interesting..." Then maybe he could be convinced.

She crossed her arms. "You won't. Not if you've been traveling all over. I've only ever been off Earth once. On a school trip to the moon."

"Earth's got a great moon," Kane said. "Did you know that the Earth is the only planet where people could see a true solar eclipse? Because of the distance of the sun and the distance of the moon are perfectly aligned to make them look the same size in the sky?"

Paris shifted in her seat and said with no eye contact, "I heard that in the old days they used to be able to see the moon nearly every night before the smog was so thick."

He'd heard that too. Kane had been to a lot of planets that humans had staked their claim on during the last century. On some, they were making the same mistakes as they had done on Earth. On others, they were trying to do better.

"Where do you want to go?" he asked again.

"I just want to see the stars."

Kane wondered if Paris was like him. If that wanderlust was in her soul too, but she had not—unlike him—had the means to feed it.

He was a man in search of interesting things, but he'd seen enough that he was starting to run low on things that could excite him. Maybe there was some novelty to be found in showing all the things he'd found to someone else— someone whose standard of amazement was just seeing the stars.

Kane raised a hand across the table for the traditional Earth gesture of a handshake.

"You got a deal."

PLANNING ADVICE FOR YOUR LAST DAYS ON EARTH

"You're not going to tell anyone. You want to know why? Because no one is going to believe you. 'I've discovered aliens! And they're on Earth! And they're planning to kill us all!'... Come on, that's the ravings of a lunatic. You'll end up incarcerated or institutionalized, depending on what you do, who you tell, and who you piss off doing it. You'll alienate — Ha! No pun intended — all your loved ones. And when you have such a short time left. See, you can't stop us. Can't fight us. Your primitive, overpopulated species doesn't have the means to escape. That's why I'm not even going to kill you. I mean, yet. You know, because of the whole plan for mass extinction thing. Because — Look, I know it's a cliché, but — resistance is futile. So, take yourself home, keep your mouth shut, and savor your last days on earth."

CREEK MONSTERS

I know that monsters exist. I know because when I was eleven years old, one tried to drown my old best friend in the creek behind my grandparents' house.

It wasn't a creek like some people call those little trickles of streams that swerve through the woods. It was a proper creek with a name on the map and everything. The houses on the other side looked as small as building blocks, and it was deep enough to dock fishing boats off of and even drown in. My grandmother never even let us go out on the end of the pier without putting on life vests from the Rubbermaid tube where she had a variety of colors and child sizes, even though both Emily and I had Girl Scout patches that proved we could swim.

Emily had the purple life vest that day. I got stuck with neon yellow.

It was early summer. The water level was high from all the rain and brown from all the storms. We sat on the edge of the pier with our legs dangling in up to the calf, minnows swimming around our toes. This was our tradition. Except when we were younger, our traditions were to play in swallow edges of the murky water, to build sandcastles on the small beach, and to scream when seaweed brushed our ankles. But since middle school, I felt awkward in a bathing suit. And earlier, Emily had said she didn't want to mess up her hair.

I don't remember what we were talking about when Emily raised one skinny leg from the water, pointing it straight out, looking like a ballerina. But I remember what she said after.

"Benji called my house yesterday."

Two opposing emotions made themselves known in my body at once: a blush to my cheeks and a sickness to my stomach.

"What for?"

"You know his birthday is over the summer."

"July 8th," I said fast and then bit my tongue. Even though it was no secret, liking a boy was still embarrassing. Or maybe the part that was embarrassing was liking a boy who didn't like you back.

"He invited me to his birthday party," Emily said.

Here's the thing about moving water. It's never just one temperature. It has warm spots and cold spots, is one thing on the surface and another thing down deep, and always shifting. Right then, a cold current wrapped around my ankles. I would realize later, it was the first sign of the monster.

"But not me." My voice felt scratchy. Don't cry, I thought, don't be a baby. We were well past our "you have to invite everyone in class" age. I needed to get past it, too.

"Do you even talk to him?" Emily dipped one leg back into the water and extended the other in the same pointed pose.

"I talked to him last year! Remember when I let him borrow my eraser —"

"You need to get over the eraser." I could hear the eye roll in her voice, even though I didn't see it.

The coldness started to crawl up.

"The party's this afternoon. That's why I have to leave early."

"But —" What about tradition? What about best friends?

"There's something else I want to talk to you about." Emily brushed a lock of her strawberry blonde hair away from her forehead. The hair she said didn't want to get messed up. The hair she didn't want to get messed up before going to Benji's party.

The coldness bloomed in my gut.

"I like Benji too."

"But —" I started, but the protests died there. The coldness grew. But what? I liked him first? More? Longer? Like any of those mattered when Emily had been invited to Benji's birthday party, and I wasn't. When Emily could speak to Benji, and I couldn't. When Emily looked like that, and I didn't. She probably didn't feel uncomfortable in a bathing suit.

"You need to be *mature* about this," she said, stretching the word like she was a decade older than our shared eleven. "We're preteens now."

She wasn't asking for my permission, sharing a secret, or commiserating on a now communal but hopeless crush. She had made her decision, and this was the aftermath. Anyone with two eyes could guess Benji or any boy in our class would pick Emily before me. But she was never supposed to compete. Best friends weren't supposed to steal your crush.

It was a painful realization that best friends forever weren't always that way. Usually weren't that way. And we hadn't so much grown apart, as I had been outgrown.

Looking back now, I know that's part of growing up. Of discovering yourself and the boundaries of your identity. With friends, with dates, with personality traits. You're not attached to the hip to one solitary friend your whole life. Had no responsibility to be.

But she didn't have to be so goddamn smug about it.

The coldness had almost completely taken over, from toe to fingertip, head to heart. Everyone thinks of anger as hot, and of monsters as loud. But anger is more like a snake: cold-blooded and lying dormant until threatened enough to strike.

Emily said something like, "It's unfair to me that I'm not allowed to like the person I like just because…" And the rest doesn't matter. My ear snagged on the word "unfair" and the monster completely took over.

My arm flew out. I didn't control it, see, the monster did. My arm flew out and grabbed the back of her perfectly clipped strawberry hair and dragged her forward. Her butt slipped off the pier, and she plunged into the creek. My elbow was locked, holding her head down under the water as she flailed and scratched at my wrist. But the monster didn't feel the pain. The monster only felt cold, cruel satisfaction.

Being pretty and popular could get you a lot of things. It couldn't save you from monsters.

But then the moment passed. The monster retreated, seeping out second by second as my control came back and I realized what I was doing as Emily's flails became weaker. I let go of her hair. The life vest — purple, my favorite color first until Emily switched hers in fourth grade — lifted her to the surface, coughing and crying.

We stopped talking, Emily and me, after that. I never got to explain the monster to her.

Never got to explain it to anyone. It's one of those things that people wouldn't believe unless they felt it themselves. The cruel creature that can crawl inside and make you do something awful. But I know. I feel it again every so often. From a cold breeze when you're bumped on the street and spill your coffee and no one apologizes. The draft in the conference room when you're talked over once, twice, a third time. When the shower turns tepid because your roommate's boyfriend used up all the hot water yet again.

I know how to curl my fingers into a fist, nails cutting tight into the palm, feeling nothing but the squeezing pain until the monster passes through, and I'm myself again, sane and sore.

Yes, I know that monsters exist.

SPIRALING

Day 9. The symbol that had been doodled onto student notebooks, magnet-ed onto refrigerator doors, dust-drawn onto dirty cars next to "clean me!" was spray-painted onto the town water tower.

Day 10. Mrs. Dawnson, widow and Sunday School teacher, called it the devil's mark to anyone who would listen, including all listeners of the WQ2 radio call-in show.

Pastor Frankfurt wasn't so explicit, but, on day twelve, gave a sermon on the dangers of vandalism and false gods.

Day 18. Lana Hixby, the proprietor of the Town Street New Age Shop, painted a spiral in the front window and made the six o'clock local news: "Children are in tune with the universe. It's all about taking our swirling inner turmoil and turning it into order."

The reporter nods with an expression of fake seriousness and cuts back to the anchor, who makes a pun and segues into the weather.

Day 32. Aaron Blackwell, a tax accountant, told his wife: "It's just the power of suggestion. Kids see other kids drawing it, then they see it on the news... of course, it's spreading." Many across Briston County, across the state, and later the country share such reasonable thoughts, but reasonable thoughts don't sell ads like CNN blasting the headline "Spiral Panic Sweeps the Nation."

Day 55. Urban Outfitters sells an off-white t-shirt with a screen-printed spiral on the front for $25.99.

Day 108. Thursday night's prime crime procedural does a thinly veiled iteration of the spiral fad, except their untimely aired production turns it into the symbol for a teen virginity-losing cult.

Day 109 to 214. An LA street artist, a Manhattan viral marketer, and two dozen drunks sprinkled across the country claim to be the originator.

Day 1462. In four years, a documentary maker will retrace the spread of the trend back to Briston County, where the spiral is still visible upon the water tower if you squint.

He doesn't find this:

Day 1. Donny Brown doodled a spiral; he wasn't much of an artist and stuck with emojis, that S-thing, and stick people. That day, a spiral was a simple thing. The canvas was a sheet of notebook paper with abandoned notes on McCarthyism.

Cara from the desk in front showed him how to make the spiral spin like the opening to the Twilight Zone by holding a pencil point down the center and flicking the corner. A quarter of the students have made their own iterations by lunchtime; anything to kick boredom out of the school day.

In seventh period, Mrs. Terry snapped, "I swear, the next spiral I see means detention…"

The rest was history.

WHAT YOU MAKE OF IT

George pressed the call button and said, "Mrs. Whitfield, you have a visitor."

Then George waited, hand resting on the phone pad, for a curt "Send them in" or the click of Mrs. Whitfield's heels in her office, or the doorknob rustling if Mrs. Whitfield deigned to open the door herself.

George smiled faintly at the waiting guest. "Overcoat" she labeled him in her head because this wasn't the weather for one. Overcoat didn't smile back, just blinked slowly, face like driftwood.

Dropping her eyes instead of engaging in a heebie-jeebie-inducing stare-off, George waited for the 3:07 in the corner of her computer screen to change over to 3:08. She couldn't buzz Mrs. Whitfield twice in less than a minute.

"George is a strange name for a young lady."

George jerked at the sound of Overcoat's creaking voice.

"I —" she glanced down at her nameplate. "Yes, it is."

"Is there a story behind it?" Overcoat asked.

George tucked an errant strand of hair behind her ear. "Isn't there always?" she said, then, "I was named after my grandfather. I was supposed to be a boy." She shrugged, tried that "oh gosh golly" grin again, the perfect disarmament.

"People aren't supposed to be anything but what they choose to be," Overcoat said, posture straight and expression unmoving.

George checked the time again. It had somehow gotten to 3:10.

"What did you say your name was again?" George resettled her finger on the call button, ready to push.

"She's expecting me," Overcoat said. "Everyone expects me at one time or another."

"Oh," George said, all she could say when being polite to Mrs. Whitfield's guests was a job requirement. "So are you like an auditor or something?"

That would make sense for the delay. George was too careful and the office phone too expensively good for the message to have gone astray. Perhaps Mrs. Whitfield was shredding incriminating paperwork as they waited — that is if Mrs. Whitfield had ever shredded her own paperwork.

"No," Overcoat said, not offended. And also not anything else.

George pressed the call button hard and spoke with an extra loud pitch, "You have a visitor."

Five seconds passed, then ten, then her phone rang. The screen showed it was an internal call from Mrs. Whitfield's office. She usually ushered commands through the intercom.

"Hello?" George said, not bothering with her corporate-generated phone pick-up spiel.

"George, can you come in here? Just you. Please," said Mrs. Whitfield, warbly, and hanging up directly after. The shocking part was the "please."

"One moment," George said to Overcoat, excusing herself as best she could into Mrs. Whitfield's office.

Mrs. Whitfield sat, hands gripping her desk's edge, as George came to stop before her, waiting for instruction.

"What's he like?" Mrs. Whitfield said, voice soft and choked up in a way George never heard from the woman before, not even as she was bedridden with pneumonia last winter, but was still commanding George and her company from the bed at a private hospital.

George racked her vocabulary for an exact word that explained the ominous but not threatening nature of Overcoat, but settled on, "He's... ah... a bit stoic."

Mrs. Whitfield nodded, leaning in, so nervous-seeming. George cocked her head, considering: Was Overcoat a gentleman caller?

Mrs. Whitfield, as anyone who read her *Forbes* bio would know, had been married and widowed early in life and in the aftermath focused solely on her career. She had been single and uninterested for as long as George had worked for her.

"He seems nice," George said, consoling and encouraging, but not entirely confident it was true.

Mrs. Whitfield cupped her hands over her mouth. "I knew it was coming, but I'm still not ready."

"Who's ever ready?" George said kindly. She was twenty-eight, with thirteen years of dating experience, and her stomach still threatened to vomit before every first date.

Mrs. Whitfield brushed her silver-gray bangs across her forehead. "I had so much more to do."

"You look great," George said. Her outfit was a bit formal for a mid-afternoon date, but the woman had never come to work looking less than immaculate, even for her many years.

Mrs. Whitfield's eyes snapped from the distant gaze beyond George's shoulder to directly on her face, eyebrows pinching in.

George flushed. Somewhere, unbeknownst to her, she'd taken a wrong turn.

"I mean... you're Evelyn Whitfield, one of the richest women in America. You've never met a person who intimidated you, let alone a man."

"You've read my memoir," Mrs. Whitfield said, recognizing the quote.

"Of course I did," George said. "Every girl I ever met in business school wanted to be you."

Mrs. Whitfield's lips curled up in a smile. "I did make an impact, didn't I?"

George nodded.

Mrs. Whitfield stood and smoothed down her pencil skirt. She stood inches over George. "I suppose there is no point in... delaying the inevitable."

George nibbled her bottom lip, keeping back advice she might have given a friend that "inevitable" was an awfully negative outlook to take on a date.

"I do appreciate you, George," Mrs. Whitfield said. "I've never said that. I don't think I should have to, considering how well I pay you, but lest it be in doubt."

George rested her palm against the desktop to steady herself, light-headed with the twists of this very odd day.

Before she exited, Mrs. Whitfield gave her skirt another smooth and said, "I'll miss it all."

George lingered in the office for a few minutes to give the couple their privacy. After she was sure she'd given them enough time to reach the elevator, she went back to her desk and redirected Mrs. Whitfield's calls until quitting time.

The next morning, George arrived at the office before Mrs. Whitfield, which was such an unusual occurrence, George could count all the times that happened on one hand.

By ten it was worrisome, by eleven George concluded Mrs. Whitfield's date must have gone really well, by noon — with no phone call — it was worrisome all over again. Worrisome enough for George to call Mrs. Whitfield's direct home line.

There was no answer. After trying it two more times, she called the front desk of Mrs. Whitfield's building.

Not her next of kin, and not one of the board members banking on her existence, George didn't get the news until a floor meeting where the CFO announced that Mrs. Whitfield had passed away last night in her sleep.

"That's so sad," Tina — the HR generalist who never had the pleasure or displeasure of working with Mrs. Whitfield directly — said beside George. "I didn't think she was that old."

"Almost seventy," George said.

"That's not old. Not anymore," Tina said as the CFO went on about how Mrs. Whitfield would be dearly missed but please do not panic during this transition period.

"What's sad is that she went on a first date last night," George said. The only date George had a hint of her going on.

She crossed her arms. Something scratched inside her skull, an understanding that couldn't quite jump across all her synapses. She was sad about Mrs. Whitfield's death, sure, but there was something more.

Tina made a puppy-like whine. "Just shows you'll never know when your time will be up. It's coming for all of us."

"Yeah," George said, as the CFO announced that the funeral details would be forthcoming. She decided the bothersome itch was a warning, that she should get back out there and have a life other than a career. What was it that Overcoat had said? She wasn't supposed to be anyone but she chose to be.

It was a good thought. Grief, like life, is what you make of it.

But it never quite satisfied George and her memories of Mrs. Whitfield's last day, like eating diet food when you're craving fat and sugar. She wouldn't figure it out until fifty-eight years later when a nurse would knock on her door at the nursing home and say, "Mrs. Dawson, you have a visitor" and it would be a man she'd nearly forgotten.

She'd know his name this time. She'd say, "I'll miss it too, but I'm ready."

ACKNOWLEDGEMENTS

Most of the short stories in this collection were previously published in literary magazines, anthologies, and journals, or on websites meant for hosting fiction. I wish to show great appreciation to the literary magazines, and their editors and staff, who first saw potential in my works and inspired me to keep writing short fiction over the years.

These publications are as follows:

- "Unfinished Business" was first published by Harbinger Press in November 2019.
- "The Pawnshop of Intangible Things"
    - Recognized by the Baltimore Science Fiction Society, which awarded it 2nd place in the 2017 Amateur Writing Contest.
    - First published by Deep Magic in the summer 2018 issue.
    - Republished in the "Short Story" Substack by Palisatrium in August 2022.
- "The Lunch Cart Diner Special" was first published in Issue 6 of The Dark Corner in fall 2021.
- "Through the Glass Darkly" was first published by Smoking Pen Press in Vampires, Zombies, and Ghosts, Volume 2 in August 2019.

- "Object Impermanence" was first published by Twenty-Two Twenty-Eight in February 2020.
- "Another Life" was first published in Future Visions, Volume 3 in August 2018.
- "Barter for the Stars" was first published by Atthis Arts in the Five Minutes at Hotel Stormcove in May 2019.
- A version of "Creek Monsters" was first published on the Simily platform in 2021.
- "Spiraling" was first published as "The Spirals" on the Tablo platform in July 2015.
- "What You Make Of It" was first published in Issue 11 of Fantasia Divinity in June 2017.

Any story not listed above is previously unpublished.

In addition, I would like to acknowledge all the family and friends who supported me throughout the creation of this collection whether it was conferring over cover designs, proofreading, sharing my posts on social media, or otherwise sharing kind words that helped motivate me in this project and in all the years of my writing journey that lead up to this point.

Last, but definitely not least, I would like to thank you, the readers, whether you know me in real life, know me through Medium or other online places, or happened to stumble across this book in some serendipitous way... Thank you. Hopefully, you enjoyed reading this as much as I enjoyed writing it.

ABOUT THE AUTHOR

Margery Bayne is a librarian by day and a writer by night from Baltimore, Maryland. She is a published author of speculative and literary short stories, and an aspiring novelist. In 2012, she graduated from Susquehanna University with a BA in Creative Writing, and continued her education to earn a Masters of Library Science from the University of Maryland in 2021. She also publishes a weekly column about short stories for The Writing Cooperative on Medium. When not reading and writing, she enjoys running, folding origami, and being the cool aunt.

More about her and her writing can be found at www.margerybayne.com.

Made in United States
Orlando, FL
18 July 2023